OTTO
and the
NEW GIRL

by Nan Walker
Illustrated by Amy Wummer

The Kane Press
New York

D1378258

Acknowledgments: We wish to thank the following people for their helpful advice and review of the material contained in this book: Susan Longo, Former Early Childhood and Elementary School Teacher, Mamaroneck, NY; and Rebeka Eston Salemi, Kindergarten Teacher, Lincoln School, Lincoln, MA.

Special thanks to Susan Longo for providing the Activities That Matter in the back of this book.

Library of Congress Cataloging-in-Publication Data

Names: Walker, Nan, author. | Wummer, Amy, illustrator.
Title: Otto and the new girl / by Nan Walker ; illustrated by Amy Wummer.
Description: New York : Kane Press, 2017. | Series: Math matters | Summary:
    In this story that introduces the math concept of symmetry, Otto and Ava
    have been best friends since discovering they both have special "mirror
    names," but Otto worries when Ava befriends new girl Vivian.
Identifiers: LCCN 2016019289 (print) | LCCN 2016047811 (ebook) | ISBN
    9781575658643 (pbk. : alk. paper) | ISBN 9781575658674 (ebook)
Subjects: | CYAC: Symmetry (Mathematics)—Fiction. | Best friends—Fiction. |
    Friendship—Fiction.
Classification: LCC PZ7.W153643 Ot 2017 (print) | LCC PZ7.W153643 (ebook) |
    DDC [E]—dc23
LC record available at https://lccn.loc.gov/2016019289

10 9 8 7 6 5 4 3 2 1

First published in the United States of America in 2017 by Kane Press, Inc.
Printed in China

MATH MATTERS is a registered trademark of Kane Press, Inc.

Visit us online at **www.kanepress.com**

 Like us on Facebook
facebook.com/kanepress

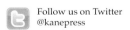 Follow us on Twitter
@kanepress

"**O**tto, you need to finish up!" my mother says. "You're going to be late for school!"

Carefully I cut my sandwich down the middle. It's my favorite, tomato and avocado. One side for me, one side for my best friend, Ava.

Perfect!

Ava and I have been friends since kindergarten, when we realized that we both have special names. If you split them down the middle, they look like a reflection in a mirror.

Symmetry is when a shape can be folded in half so that both sides are perfect mirror reflections of each other. The names OTTO and AVA are symmetrical when they are written in capital letters.

Now we split everything right down the middle. Sneakers. Coloring books. Even the flu.

And, of course, sandwiches.

But when Ava comes over to our cafeteria table, she is with a girl I've never seen before.

"This is Vivian," Ava says, "the new girl in my class. I'm showing her around."

I say hi, then pass Ava half my sandwich.

"Ooh!" Vivian says. "I love avocado!"

Ava smiles. "Want to trade?"

Just like that, Vivian has half of *my* sandwich. Ava has half of Vivian's lasagna. And I have half of Ava's peanut butter and banana wrap.

I don't even like bananas.

The **line of symmetry** is the line where you can fold an image and have each half match exactly.

When we go out for recess, Ava asks, "Want to play on the monkey bars?"

"Sure!" Vivian says.

"But we always go on the seesaw!" I protest.

"Only two of us can use the seesaw at a time," Ava explains. "And there are three of us today."

Line of symmetry

First bananas. Now the monkey bars.

I feel like Curious George. Only I'm not curious. I'm just confused. Why is Ava acting as if this new girl is her best friend? Does she like Vivian better than me?

Everything is upside down.

It seems like the longest recess ever. But at last the bell rings and we line up to go inside.

Ava's teacher smiles at the girls. "Vivian, I see we picked a good 'buddy' to show you around."

Vivian grins back, and so does Ava.

Suddenly I'm smiling too.

Of course! That's why Ava's spending so much time with Vivian. She's her "buddy," not her new best friend.

When school lets out, Ava and I will go to my house and do homework, just like any other day.

But after school, Ava and Vivian come out
together, giggling over Ava's notebook.

"Otto, look!" Ava says. "Viv has a mirror
name, too, just like us!"

I want to say, *But mirror names are* our *thing!*
Instead I say, "But . . . her real name is Vivian."

Ava smiles. "She says we can call her Viv."

"Want to come over and watch Power Pets?" Vivian asks us. "I've got the episode where Iron Penguin first meets Major Pig."

"We've been dying to see that one!" Ava says, just as I say, "No, thanks."

Ava shoots me a surprised look.

"Oh, well, then . . . see you later!" Ava says.

She's not talking to Vivian. She's talking to me.

I walk home alone.

I can't believe my best friend would abandon me for a cartoon.

Even if it is the greatest cartoon ever.

I bet they're having a fantastic time.

At home I get out my Power Pets action figures. I can have fun all by myself.

"Iron Penguin is *my* sidekick!" Major Pig snorts angrily.

Evil Mutant Monkey growls, "MINE!"

They fight until Iron Penguin loses a flipper. I guess he isn't made of iron after all.

Symmetrical   Asymmetrical

Maybe I should have gone with Ava.
I try to call her, but she's still not home.

"Who needs a best friend, anyway?" I ask.
Then I realize I'm talking to myself.
I sigh. "Me, that's who."

The next morning, I decide I'm going to win Ava back.

I pack her favorite lunch—mac and cheese.

Today we're meeting in the auditorium to work on props for our third grade play.

I sit down next to an empty seat and call out, "Ava! Over here!"

Ava waves. "Come sit with Viv and me!"

I look. Vivian has the middle seat. Why does she keep coming between Ava and me?

"But I like *these* seats," I say desperately.

Ava looks puzzled. I want her to say, "Otto, you're still my best friend. I'll sit with you."

Instead, she shrugs and sits down.

Our teachers go over the rules about Being Responsible with Paint. Then they tell us to pair up and choose a cardboard prop to paint.

I slump. Ava will pair up with Vivian, I bet. And I'll be left alone.

"Otto, want to paint the lizard?"

It's Ava! She wants to work with me!
"Ooh," Vivian says. "I love lizards!"
Quickly I say, "We have to work in pairs."
"You and Viv can work together!" Ava says.
"I'll go paint the cactus with Abdul."

"What color should we paint it?" Vivian asks. "Green, like a gecko? Or we could give it a blue tail, like a skink."

I draw a pencil line straight down the middle. "You paint your side," I say. "I'll paint mine."

Some shapes have no lines of symmetry, some shapes have one line of symmetry, and some shapes have several lines of symmetry!

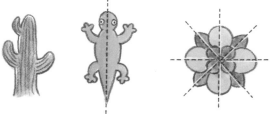

My teacher comes and stands over us.

"That lizard certainly is . . . *different*," he says.

My side of the lizard is striped. Vivian's has spots and three new cardboard horns. It's different, all right—and *weird*.

I wait for Vivian to tell him it was all my fault. Instead she says, "Ooh! It's an evil mutant lizard. I *love* evil mutant stuff!"

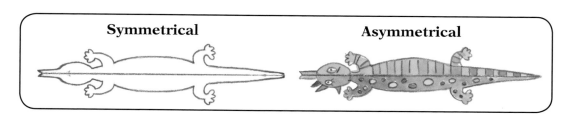

Symmetrical   **Asymmetrical**

"You do?" I ask.

Vivian nods. "Evil Mutant Monkey is my absolute favorite Power Pet."

"Really?" I say. "Mine too!"

She smiles. I hesitate, then smile back.

At lunch I see Ava and Vivian sitting together.

"Otto!" Vivian calls out. "Over here!"

I sit down and spoon the mac and cheese into two cups.

"Ooh!" Vivian says. "I love mac and cheese."

"You can have mine," Ava offers.

But it's her favorite lunch!

"No!" I say. "You can have *my* half . . . Viv."

Vivian laughs. "I don't want anybody's half."

"You don't?" I ask.

Viv shakes her head. "There are three of us. Let's split everything three ways."

And just like that, I have the best lunch ever—and *two* friends to share it with.

After lunch we wait for Viv to bus her tray.

"Viv is great!" I tell Ava. "I was worried that I wasn't your best friend anymore. But I had it all backward. We can stay friends and have a new friend too."

"Of course!" Ava says.

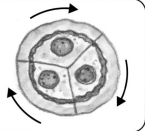

Bonus!
Rotational symmetry is different from regular symmetry. It happens when a shape looks exactly the same after it's been rotated.

At recess we all go on the merry-go-round. With three of us, we get it spinning really fast.

I feel super happy, and I know it isn't just the ride.

I'm glad the three of us can all be friends—
without anyone in the middle!

SYMMETRY CHART

What is symmetry?

When a shape is folded in half on the line of symmetry and the two sides line up perfectly, then the shape is **symmetrical**. It has **symmetry**.

Here are some examples of shapes that are **symmetrical**.

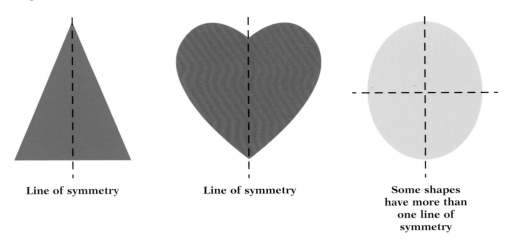

Line of symmetry   Line of symmetry   Some shapes have more than one line of symmetry

Here are examples of shapes that are not symmetrical (or **asymmetrical**). These shapes have no symmetry.

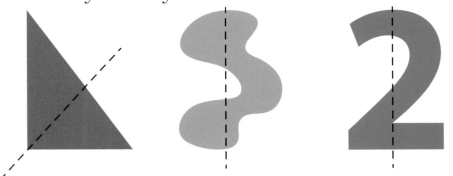